White Sheets

Beverley Bie Brahic is a poet and translator. A Canadian, she lives in Paris and Stanford, California. Her translation of selected poems by Francis Ponge, *Unfinished Ode to Mud* (CBe, 2008) was shortlisted for the 2009 Popescu Prize for European poetry in translation. In early 2012 CBe published her translations of poems by Apollinaire under the title *The Little Auto*.

Of Beverley Bie Brahic's previous collection, *Against Gravity* (2005), George Szirtes wrote: 'I doubt whether we will see a more sensuous book, with as much control as this, for a good while, nor one written as lightly, with as little apparent effort. But that, of course, is the secret.'

also by Beverley Bie Brahic

POETRY
Against Gravity

TRANSLATIONS
Guillaume Apollinaire, *The Little Auto*
Francis Ponge, *Unfinished Ode to Mud*
Hélène Cixous, *Hemlock*
Hélène Cixous, *Hyperdream*
Hélène Cixous, *Manhattan*
Hélène Cixous, *Dream I Tell You*
Hélène Cixous and Roni Horn, *Agua Viva* (*Rings of Lispector*)
Hélène Cixous, *The Day I Wasn't There*
Hélène Cixous, *Reveries of The Wild Woman*
Hélène Cixous, *Portrait of Jacques Derrida as a Young Jewish Saint*
Jacques Derrida, *Geneses, Genealogies, Genres and Genius*
Julia Kristeva, *This Incredible Need to Believe*

OTHER
the eye goes after
(limited edition artist's book of digital images by Susan Cantrick
accompanying poems by Beverley Bie Brahic)

Beverley Bie Brahic

WHITE SHEETS

First published in 2012
by CB editions
146 Percy Road London W12 9QL
www.cbeditions.com

Printed in England by Blissetts, London W3 8DH

ISBN 978–0–9567359–5–9

for
Catherine, François,
Anne, Jon and Lucie

Acknowledgements

Thanks to the editors of the following publications where poems in this collection, some of them in earlier versions and with other titles, first appeared: *Ambit*, *Bellevue Literary Review*, *The Bow Wow Shop*, *Field*, *Literary Imagination*, *The Malahat Review*, *Measure*, *London Magazine*, *The North*, *Notre Dame Review*, *Oxford Poetry*, *PN Review*, *Poetry* (Chicago), *A Public Space*, *The Southern Review*, *Times Literary Supplement*, *Verse*, *Verse Daily*.

'Disposable' ('A Crate'), 'The Oyster' and 'Blackberries' appear in Francis Ponge, *Unfinished Ode to Mud* (London, CB editions, 2008, trans. Beverley Bie Brahic). 'The Cigarette' is from Francis Ponge, *Le parti pris des choses* (*Oeuvres complètes*, Paris, Gallimard, 1999). 'Three Paintings by Poussin' is from Yves Bonnefoy, *La longue chaîne de l'ancre* (Paris, Mercure de France, 2008).

Immense gratitude to the Canada Council for the Arts for its grant, the Corporation of Yaddo for its gift of time at Saratoga Springs, and the generous friends who read these poems in draft.

Contents

WHITE SHEETS

HORTUS NOT CONCLUSUS

IN MY MOTHER'S GARDEN

WHITE SHEETS

White Sheets

Airstrike hits wedding party – breaking news

The empty laundry basket
fills with molecules of light.
She stands beside it, arms falling
into the aftermath of the task.
Gesture is a proto-language
researchers say: the same circuits
light the brain when a chimp
signals help me please (hand
outstretched, palm up) as when
human beings process speech.
In the cave the hunter figure
mirrors his spear's trajectory
towards the deer it will never,
of course, attain. The woman
sees nothing untoward. Her body
bars the spattered something
in the middle distance, though all
of this is right up close: the shed
they'll use to dress the meat, the plane
geometry of white sheets
on a line. The world is beautiful,
she thinks, or feels, as deer
sense something coming
and move out of range. Beautiful,
the woman thinks, and lifts
the laundry basket to her arms –
beautiful, and orderly.

Ancient History

I

Sixty years after D-Day, in a week
of sunshine and occasional rain,
my quiet father died: a small
civilian hospital, Canada's west coast.
The staff deployed their arsenal –
ice chips, morphine.
He'd have felt fortunate, though
he rarely spoke of it, he returned
from that war, much of it spent, the citation
says, 'well forward . . . evacuating
casualties' (from Latin *casus* – meaning chance,
meaning the less fortunate ones).
Mother and daughter, we watched
the body's last fight to survive,
scanned columns of heartbreak
dropped on our doorstep at dawn,
or stared out a dusty window
past some fruit from the garden – food
for the rest of the journey,
offering to whoever the gods.

Waging war is safer now
leaner faster surgical teams
accompany the troops, vehicles
fitted with sterile instruments,
operating tables, anaesthesia
     and the
Deployable Rapid Assembly
Shelters – acronym *DRASH* –

nowadays, this surgeon reports
in a prominent medical journal,
just one wounded soldier in 10 will die.

Open to the centrefold: spine
crushed by a roadside device –
nails, bolts and the bones
of his assailant – with injuries
unsurvivable in previous wars
this soldier won't be *numbered*
among the fallen

(wince at the consecrated words,
and a *fallen woman*, what's that,
and a *boy*, cannon fodder or house slave?):

taped together like old script,
medevacked to mother, to spouse

maybe what Pericles meant
when he told the Athenians

heroes don't need monuments
heroes have the whole earth for their tombs.

III

I rest my book on its spine;
stir the apricots I purchased for jam,
a crateful at the market this morning.
The last of them, the stall-holder said.

After the first season of the Peloponnesian War
wheat threshed, grain stored in silos,
grapes pressed to dark wine

the Athenians bury their dead.

Thucydides records their rituals

The bones of the dead laid in chests
of cypress wood
still smelling of trees

are borne to a monument in the finest part
of the city. A citizen – that first winter
they asked Pericles – delivers an oration

mourners bring offerings
the women come to lament . . .

How solid the world of the Athenians – I think –
watching fruit bubble
in the hand-me-down preserving kettle –

you'd think this had all happened yesterday.

Disposable

Halfway from *cage* to *dungeon*, the French language has *crate,* a simple slatted box for carrying such fruits as at the least lack of air are sure to wilt.

Knocked together so that when it's no longer needed it can be easily crushed, it's not used twice. Which makes it even less durable than the juicy or cloudlike produce it contains.

Then, at the corner of every street leading to the market-place, it gleams with the modest sparkle of deal. Still brand new and a little dazed to find itself in the street in such an awkward pose, cast off once and for all, this object is on the whole one of the most appealing – on whose destiny however there's little point to dwell.

after Francis Ponge

Goya: 'The Fight with Cudgels'

They face off in the mud. Neither brother
will survive. In fact they're already dead.
Knee deep in mud, in that welter
like the dog – Goya's hapless pup – wedded
to whatever the matter is: sky aglow
as over Crete that evening, Easter
weekend, Straw Man roped to his scaffold,
vine shoots heaped, kids fondle Bic lighters;
Processions, Ejaculations, Carnations,
the Matrons lined up to kiss the icons.
In every household, lamb offal simmers.
But these two clubbing each other?
Cadmus sowed the dragon's teeth. Armed
they rose and killed their brother. No one won.

Reunion: J-School, Class of 19—

Cutlery clatters into the sink.
But always the characters, uniquely themselves,
only some decades older. They search
for their coats. You were, she reminds him,
our resident nomad, come to pitch your tent
here, sidewalks for sand, unaccustomed taboos:
Morningside Heights, one of your lives.
                              Thirty years
since the awkward goodbye? Before he goes –
East Africa his beat, Germany hers – he'll
visit the nephew, the namesake in Boston
who drives a cab, sends a pittance each month
to a wellhead in – we'll call it *Sudan*.
He explains how it works, this drip feed
of cash to *Sudan* from the *United States*:
cheap, fast. She's not clear about this – he jots
her a website: it's a place she can go.
So they won't meet again . . . suddenly
Can you forgive me? he blurts –
a classmate's apartment, Upper West Side,
the grown child's room, bears
in tidy shrines, scrum of sloughed coats.
In the kitchen friends wash up. Sound
of laughter. Sound of water flowing
out of a tap. *Yes,* she replies, shocked
by the twinge, then ache, of remorse.
She '*forgot*'? And him – thirty years –
the place still hurts? *It's myself I can't forgive,*
she knows later. Right now, vague shame.

End of *March*. Maybe *April*. Street trees
try to bloom. The irretrievable
sits on the table, white as a plate. He holds her
her coat.

On the Pathetic Fallacy

A bird bangs your window – no tender lamb,
no Corinna, just you
with your feet up, Reader, reading, and a sheet of glass
between you, the tree
and the carport's tarpaper roof. It's a real bird
(now you hunt
for its name): it's a *genus* something
species something, it's not some despair of your own
masquerading as a bird.
Bigger than a sparrow, with a black hood. Beak dipped
in egg yolk.
Body two-tone, like a fifties Chevrolet – here it is, Reader,
you found it! *Junco
hyemlis* (16 cm [6¼ in] long).

Why does this '*Junco hyemlis*'
(if that's its name) keep
thrashing at the pane? Another bird, a bird
it doesn't know
is a double of itself? Reflection,
rival, or a mate,
another Junco on a winter branch of the birch
tree at your window,
near the carport roof? Wave your arms,
Reader, shout! No good. You're trapped
behind glass, in a box, in far away
repeat repeat repeat repeat repeat repeat repeat repeat repeat re-
why should it ever stop?

Jingle Pot Road

His heart was on the blink again.
He shrugged it off long distance
with his usual modesty. Sunday
morning on their coast; in Paris
the sun was down.

                No church, a deluge,
cormorants doing their submarine thing.
So that's the news – oh – Wednesday –
he has a check-up on the mainland,
they'll take a peek at that pig valve . . .
puts me off my eggs and bacon.

Dad skipped town on me. Shipped overseas
and left me swimmy: mother's belly.
I have his wallet, with the snapshots,
each milk tooth logged in mother's hand:
first steps . . . second birthday candle . . .
                I forget dad's demob.
Remember the Hans Brinker skates,
a German officer's scabbard and sword.

       . . .

Interminable, flights home – I doze
and wake, peer down the airshaft
of space at shadows thrown across Arctic ice
          – Greenland, Baffin –
what on earth time is it down there?
In Paris, night falls without haste; starlings

flock to the oak. A neighbour appears on her porch,
gives her white cloth
a conjurer's shake. Crumbs, crumbs.
Down come the starlings.

. . .

In hip waders and torn gloves
dad peers through a lens of water.
In the tide-pool, the heron is back,
patient as a fly fisherman. 'Here,'
he says – half shell of brine, blob
of flesh laced with blood.
How come we've got this crummy knife?
Same old questions, back like flotsam:
his Depression prairie boyhood,
a world war that came between us.

Neither of us has the gift of the gab.
We stare at our toes and come up
with oysters, crusted in barnacles.
He knows a great place for the fish and chips
I still hanker for – the buoyant deep-fry,
salt, vinegar. Tonight, long distance,
he says it again –
there's a new fish and chip shop,
it's down where the ferries dock,
it's off Jingle Pot Road.

The Oyster

The oyster, big as a good-sized pebble, is less regular in appearance, in colour less uniform, dazzlingly whitish. A world stubbornly closed. Still it can be opened: cup it in a tea towel, use a notched but fairly blunt knife, keep at it. Curious fingers get cut at this game, nails break: it's rough work. Our jabs mark it with white rings, sorts of halos.

Inside you find a whole world, to eat and to drink: beneath a *firmament* (strictly speaking) of mother-of-pearl, the heavens above slump into the heavens below, forming a pond, a viscous greenish blob, which ebbs and flows in our eyes and nose, in its fringe of blackish lace.

Once in a while a formula seeds itself in the mother-of-pearl gullet, upon which we seize, to adorn ourselves.

after Francis Ponge

[15]

Receiving Qi Baishi's 'Longevity Peaches' on a Postcard from a Friend

Two peaches – a proof of ripeness –
in your thief's hand.
Why do the Chinese paint trees, bark,
rocky precipices, rarely portraits?
History is painting's highest form,
our Renaissance said. The body
in motion, raping a few Sabines.
Images of the powerful and/or seductive.
A woman posed on a couch,
painter poised to toss his palette
and have her. Even Chardin alludes
to the figure who stepped out, leaving
the fruit untasted, the kitchen knife.
Carmine, these peaches that thrust
from foliage, to honour the master
on his sixtieth birthday.
Or (Zhejiang says), 'the red flowers
demand the contrast of green leaves.'

Three Paintings by Poussin

His tomb, you ask? But it's this place
he left hollow, deep in the foliage
of the tree where old Apollo muses
on what's young, and so more than god.

And it's also this chink of light
in the *Birth of Bacchus*, when the sun
takes hope, unblemished, in his hands,
and with it paints the sky that changes.

His tomb? What this stern gaze sees
unravelling, deep in the *Self-Portrait*
whose silver, that loved his dream, dulls:

an old man, at evening, astonished,
but still determined to say the colour,
late, his hand become a mortal thing.

after Yves Bonnefoy

Solstice

Shortest day
of the year, almost.
Redwood tip
bedraggled as the pelican
feather you scavenged
from the beach.
The pomegranates
split, they spit seed
underfoot. Crisp
taffeta of leaves wrens
tussle in – see, just
what's here. Look

at this kitchen
from Chardin! burnished
kettle upended on
a slab of wood; an
earthen bowl (big
enough to beat
two eggs) glazed
umber brown. Erect
in its wooden fist,
the pestle. A knife
pares the shadow
of a red onion.

Behind, Before . . .

Above derelict mailboxes bolted
to a rotting post weathered silky grey,
one flapping open (nothing to hide),
the other askew, steel bullet-pocked;

across from the gutted barn, fridge
carcass, cardboard boxes' mulch of papers,
weeds jimmying through the concrete
where horses flicked flies from their flanks;

under the curve of sunburnt hills
greening in a spizzle of January rain,
fog sliding down like the goose-down quilt

you yank up in the small cold hours
as your bare thigh
searches the bedclothes for his:

that mimosa's about to erupt into buttery bloom.

One Orange

It's on waking sex is best.
On padded paws the pack of dreams retreats
without a backward look to memorise
the undulations in terrain – impress the brain
with how their route will look
tonight when they come back
the other way. No wonder they get lost.
A hand reaches out, reaches down.
Locates the spring where water starts.
Outside, one orange bobbles on the tree.
It's on waking sex is best.

Conkers

Good for curing what-ails-you
old wives profess. Chestnuts –
she thinks them found coin

jingling in pockets of leaf mulch
of the old stag hunting grounds,
their *Oratoires de la pucelle.* Folly's ruins?

Deer eat them
without harm.
They cure wind in horses.

Serve as weapons for kids.
Placed in corners of rooms
they keep spiders out.

Ripe, their cases split
tumbledown prickly blow-open wedge
gleam of mahogany brown –

like this wife's best view of her husband
(your classic bent-over backside bedtime view):
the fork in his trunk,

round touchstones
to heat the pan
of your hand, a trail

of crumbs
to the snow-whitish sheets.

On Stendhal's Pants

Stendhal, my dear, you were saying
as we biked back from the pond (fireflies
   fizzing in the leaves),
scribbled thoughts around the waistband
of his pants, in hopes, you said, his words
would rub off on his skin. 'Around
his trousers?' I clarified. 'You don't think
he wore underwear?' Your brow arched. Flustered,
I let my question drop.

   Esprit d'escalier. What I wish I'd said,
dear scholar, is that my reading
of eighteenth-century erotic tales, a plumpish volume
whose Watteau cover girl perches,
                panniers hitched,
on a spindly chair astride a gentleman
who, for all I know, may be deep
              in thought
about the oysters, delectable, the trio
that accompanied them – unless, that is,
the gentleman's a scribbler, attending to the friction
of his thoughts against his skin (the way an oyster tends
its grain of sand) – leads me to think
in those days *no one* wore underwear
(that complication not unlike the lace
of clauses that defer thought's resolution) –

quoique . . . cher maître . . . I confess
this may be a case of wishful thinking
on the part of Gentle Reader, prompt –
                             too prompt? –
to take words for reality.

Eve to Her Daughters:
Thou Shalt Not Commit Adultery

Actually not that easy to commit –
primo you need an Other Man, sexy
goes without saying – not *too* young, the Rake
who'll play Temptation to your Vamp.

Next you need a spark, like God's forefinger
    stretched across the vault

or the first time I and Adam,
    my one and only
husband, love's First Cause and template,
rubbed our two sticks of kindling together –
    whoosh! – first my brush-
then his pine-wood burst into flame.

Say these conditions are met – it happens,
believe me – next stoke the blaze:
it ought to seem spontaneous.
    This is the tough part.
Fan the flames, but be covert; when they're hot
concoct some errand to run:
    some excuse to head
into the woods. Mind you've cash – don't
want the chits from Paradise Inn & Lounge
    coming home to roost.

A word to the wise,
daughters: if the deed requires airplane tickets,
disguise and getaway car I'm afraid
    it's just not on –

But hey! Can't a lady dream? You'll be glad
you've got your secret rooms and
key cards, when you and your Adam
    snuggle up this evening
by the embers, on your grizzly rug.

But girls, forgive me, I have to run,
I've got a date for lunch at – you know –
that place along the Seine: *Malmaison*,
Bougival, *Louveciennes*, *Le Port Marly*,
where rooms I hear are going
for 42 euros, or 45 with a river view
and half a dozen dirty swans.

The Cigarette

First let us render the atmosphere, both hazy and dry – dishevelled – in which the cigarette reclines, all the while creating it.

Then the personage: a tiny torch, less luminous than fragrant, from which a calculable number of small ash heaps drop at a rate as yet to be determined.

Lastly, the passion for it: this fiery button sloughing off its silvery scales, cuffed by the most recent ones.

after Francis Ponge

Book of Eve: Chapter 44

Theocritus, *Puerilities*, freely

44 Across the veranda, he shot me a look
and night after night for weeks I tossed in his arms
in my head. Didn't he give me a pat
when he left – to go where? – with whoever
she thinks she is with her whippet waist and come-hither gait.
    A pilot light, she's always lit. No
wonder he jumped. 'Fool!' I fume. 'Your wrinkles
have wrinkles. Your hair? – mostly salt.
Should be cooking up jam, not some soap opera plot.'

But oh! the muss of his curls! At the nape!
What he needs is a trim. A woman
to take him in hand, show him what women like.
I saw him wince when the breeze tweaked my skirt. Didn't
    he fetch me wine? Paper plate
of crisps? Before Ms What's-Her-Name
swept in – 'if you want to (to *what?*) come now' –
he leapt like he'd sat on a bee, though he
remembered to give me a pat, promise
he'd finish telling me about his acid trip
                some other time.

Think I will buy that dress, black, plunge-neck. Paint
my toenails blood. Might as well count stars, or
    cow parsley along the back roads
as reckon up the odds against my making it with him.
Obsess, obsess. Sure, I know I'm a fool. But tell me,
where's an end to this ache – this itch – this delight
in falling, in love?

Her Pedicure

Postmodern Eve has learned to deconstruct
    her erogenous zones: alcove
of the ear, teacup breast, but best –
    this button on its silken sleeve.

So far Eve hasn't counted on her toes
    though once, in a museum shop, she glimpsed
a Chinese picture book whose
    concubines' trim toes entranced.

But dream she moonlights at the old profession –
    for one wild afternoon can
Eve indulge her inner courtesan?
    Eve's easily undone by Man.

Cut to the Paris scene. Off *Rue de B—*,
    Place de la Concorde: mirrors, chic
robes, urns of crumpled peonies,
    one blotted with a lipstick streak.

The camera's roving eye zooms in:
    Eve's rosy nails Seduction files
and buffs and paints a shade of crimson
    Eve finds irresistible

                    and falls.
                    Again.

On the Road to the Mont Ventoux

By evening we reached the foot of the Mont Ventoux – Petrarch

Pure chance. Say
some fruit left on a cherry tree
along the road
to the trailhead

where you shrugged your pack
off into scruff,
and looked back
towards the village – church

skewed towards a graveyard
calm as a kitchen garden –
folded leeks, a dozen
staked tomato vines.

Say a stranger on the platform
of a station – Avignon, was it? –
with whom you trade
badinage. Nameless small birds

decamp, take their quarrels
up the road – truffle oaks. Cherries,
tiny, wild: pebbles
of memory, like ones

we leave on graves
to remember us by. Not much
flesh on the stones.
But good – *aigrelette* –

hereabouts they pick
them, if they pick them,
to distill
a kind of eau de vie –

we'll take a capful
for the trail, this old sheep track
to a summit Petrarch,
with his pockets full

of Augustine's *Confessions*,
also set off one day to climb.

Teapot

Daughters are the guardians of memory,
said *Belle-maman*, spooning bread with honey.

– And why not sons? But to her daughters
she left the linens, darned with memories.

I've flown home from the other country, over
my native provinces the colour of honey.

Farewell for a while to the rented condo,
kitchen cupboards unfurnished with memories.

I lift the teapot – the Aladdin-shaped one –
down from the shelf, and the jar of honey.

A wedding gift. Often dropped. Lid askew,
pewter blotched. The soft cloth of memory

makes it a lamp on the dullest day, a mirror
with tarnished silvering. I drizzle honey

over my bread. Kettle chirps. I warm the pot.
I steep verbena in the teapot of memory.

What if I swaddle it like a hot water bottle,
pack it up with a jar of the lavender honey,

fly it some Great Circle Route back to Silicon Valley,
my kitchen cupboards, bare of memories?

Then, if I fly northeast again, over
my native forests, prairies and honey,

I'll leave it with my son – no – my daughter:
daughters are the guardians of memory,

and my son will fall in love with another woman
(I see her already; she's a honey)

and will she, won't she
care for my memories?

Yardwork

The last of the grapes, those even wasps
disdain, cling to the bottom squiggle of vines, puckered,
       sun-dried, sweet as raisins,
fermenting, edible almost-wine: we nibble them
weeding under the mulberry tree, yanking up tufts
of asparagus fern, spears of wild leek. The earth soft
after rain, roots come easily, a mound of them
       from white, sharp-stony
dirt. I tidy the base of the butterfly bush whose white
panicles and silver-backed leaves bob when bees dipped in pollen
       land, and drone off
like overloaded planes; the branches bend, they bounce,
they rest.

From the attic, once a granary (house against a hill,
front door two floors down), we unfold origami chairs. Dazed,
       drunk, our tools
slump against a wall: the rake, a shovel, pitchfork, blunt
shears. A hose snakes across flagstones to a trough
for the horse no longer stabled here; and the watering can
       (white-enamelled great aunt)
purses its lip. Below, above the village cemetery, a chapel,
stone blind with heat. Honeysuckle – blowzy
as a woman out of bed. She yawns, squints at the sun
       glinting off the olive trees;
barefoot, she pads downstairs. Puts the singing kettle on.

HORTUS NOT *CONCLUSUS*

Carpaccio's Dog

You were startled to find trees in Venice –
to turn the corner into that campo
where two or three rustling acacias
spread their halo of leaves
over two or three red-slatted benches –
as if you'd ducked through a portal
into a hall full of dull gold scenes
by Carpaccio – a miraculous light –
though the bridge's hump back still hunkered
in a mist of water vapour and smog
so it wasn't that the sun had come out –
it had something to do with the trees

and painting, in a city where footsteps
resound endlessly behind walls, where dawn
is the chink of a stonemason
at his reparations, disembodied voices
irrepressible as bird calls. It was like
Carpaccio's little white dog, its head
cocked at Augustine, who stares at his window
– panes ruddy with sun – stunned
to hear the voice of Saint Jerome.
What was it, about those trees (in Venice)
shedding their gold leaf onto the pavement
outside the secondhand bookstore?

The Annunciations

1 *Bellini*

From our *pensione* we spy
    children at play, monitored
        by nuns, a convent whose cordial

walls (plaster sloughing off
    corroded brick) frame a cloister's
        recurrent paths.

Shutters slam. Sun floods
    a neighbour's apartment,
        she – in just a towel – caught

off guard, then a gold
    curtain cancels the scene.
        How Bellini must have loved

the Virgin's shock, crumpled metal
    (auto body, compacted) of Gabriel's
        robe, the flower, hyperreal,

as he (angel, messenger, lusty
    god) glides into the atrium
        – and her recoil.

2 *Santa Maria Assunta*

Climbed the Campanile, my Cate and I – needle
    flash of lagoon, gardens
  wild, lace tablemats and christening
      robes crocheted like webs.

Hear the ferry's wake slosh against piles?
    Effect of an angel
  receding into café walls? Wasps over windfalls.
      Due cappuccini,

signore, per favore. Mary spills the yarn, heart
    does a flop – needles
  pins bobbins spools eels
      of thread in all directions – but where

oh where, can Mary run? I mean the lace,
    I mean the knots – I mean
  the sun against these bricks;
      today is almost warm.

The Dome Web

Not a piece of lacework laid out to dry, filaments
    tensile in sun – not a tightrope
tossed from point a to point b across a dry gulch
      of nothingness (spindly Joshua tree) – not even
a safety net, guy wires taut
    to catch a trapezist out of the sky, Icarus

star-spangled in gravity. No – nothing
    so predictable. Not your dew-studded orb at dawn
when sunlight touches it, but a chart
      of the infinitesimal
space of the revolving screen – a synapse
    creating the world in its image –

a web in the woods on Thormanby Island!
    String-theory-dimensional. A dome web, soap
bubble alight on a catwalk of needles, rusty bracken,
      apparatus of twigs; a snarl
    of fly-fishing line you itch to untangle
with your clumsy, prehensile fingers, to track

its erotic thread down, into the labyrinth, black-
    berry brambles, tuft of weeds, shafts of light – with Ariadne,
      or Arachne the impenitent,
confined to her loom – her crime lèse majesté –
    taking things as they come,
bluebottles breezes waspish goddesses

Blackberries, Blackberries, Blackberries

On the typographic bushes of the poem down a road leading neither out of things nor to the mind, certain fruits are
composed of an agglomeration of spheres plumped with a drop
of ink.

. . .

Black, pink and khaki together on the bunch, they look like
a rogue family, all ages: scarcely a temptation to pick.

So many seeds! So little pulp! Birds haven't much use for
them, so little remains once from beak to anus they've been
traversed.

. . .

But the poet, on his walk, takes the seed to task: 'So,' he
tells himself, 'the dogged efforts of a fragile flower on a rebarba-
tive tangle of brambles are by and large successful. Not much to
recommend them, but – *ripe*, no denying they're ripe – like my
poem.'

after Francis Ponge

In My Mother's House

Grown – still trying to please Mother.
Don't leave dishes in the sink
I entreat. People, chairs – I set
them straight. Sweep nothing under rugs.

Atlantics and a continent away
she's much too old to disapprove of what I do
(write this! what a lie!):
still I cower like a child, afraid

Mother will come storming
to my room – so clean! – to find again
what a mess of things I've made.

. . .

*I think I had the happiest childhood
a child could have*, she says that dusk.
Side by side we drink her scotch
and watch the mainland fade,

me – bemused to hear her praise. And
shouldn't happy childhoods be passed on
        like the shapely legs
and granddad's tall case clock?

One more thing I must record, mom said
when we tidied up his things: Zeiss
binoculars he brought back, medals

buried in a drawer, the little pile
of library books not yet expired:
All our wedded life I felt
I wasn't good enough to be his wife.

Mother, did I
get everything wrong? And
    what of love – that word
we've never learned to say?

Hortus not Conclusus

In the depiction of the Last Judgement
whose comic strip perspectives enlighten
this cathedral, when the wrecked souls
approach the Blessed Isles
the guardian angels are there with poles
to turn them away. They bob
in flames, like boat people.
Mary holds out her arms beseechingly,
but mourning is her default mode.

One of the tourists, I can't stop staring
at the figures relegated
to the bottom frames.
They haven't any private parts.

High up, the Blessed, with here and there
a finger raised, a bunch of keys.
There's Eve waiting to be judged,
swathed head to toe in scarlet –
elder daughter shamed for disobeying
the parent who said *just because*.
She keeps her plucky hands tucked
into her sleeves; or maybe –
maybe – they were lopped
to teach the girl a lesson for daring
to dream beyond the garden walls.
In stiff gold folds the Patriarchs
blend with the wall-to-wall mosaic.

Ear pressed to the audio guide, I let
my eyes drift down the chips of clay,
       the *tesserae*,
down the Blessed and to-be-Blessed
(it's the game of Snakes and Ladders
we played as kids, before the advent
of Monopoly), across each strip
of frozen time, to the astonished
bodies discovering their nakedness

Compost

Growing dark in the Paris suburb
when I uncover the toad, dull splotch
a pulse, fluttering. I crouch –
I won't hurt you, I say. Tell dad,
I think. Bait wriggles in the hole.

All afternoon I dug: teetering,
shuddering wheelbarrow loads. Years
of rot dumped on the beds.
Tell dad – I think – tell him finally
I got around to the job.

Of course, I'm forgetting dad's dead
and that he would never pick up
the phone: *I'm always afraid
there'll be somebody there.*

I set the toad back under some leaves
where my bantams – copper-coloured hen
and her bonfire mate – liked to peck.
If I forgot them they'd roost in the boughs
but they crowed in my sleep – and the cats!
But a bantam – oh, it's a fancy-dress hat
with an extravagant plume – and when
I pulled them from the branch I had nothing
in my arms – a beating heart
baffled by all the seasons of leaves.

It was August dad died: next breath, next
he didn't take, brief
cooling of the flesh.

We kept the fly-casting rods, tin boxes
of flies, feathery things
stored in their separate compartments,
like a woman's mending, or embroidery,
threads.

I owe Aesclepius a cock, remember
Socrates' twinge – ?

Put my ashes in the compost, dad said
philosophically. One night when the tide was slack
we scattered a portion under a rock,
the remainder over a gravelly stream –
great place, he'd have said, for trout.

Coda

Great blue heron leans on the water, a Venetian
glass figurine toeing the line of a mirror's bevel:
    he spots you
  without turning his head –

changes into a rainbow, a trout – Iris
    who eludes your grasp
in the pool of another rock, aloof
  as a goddess looping her scarf.

Her periscope is his gooseneck, slinky,
    sex-flexible. Shuffles into a backwards S,
squashed to a U-bend, plunges rapidly in
    and out again – the mirror

breaks, shards of bottle-glass jag the wall:
    Danger! Keep Out!
The surface calms. Great blue won't
  give you a nod.

When it stalks, it goes gingerly, lifts
  one articulate stilt, the second. Its eye
juts ahead of it. Its reflection
    shadows it, a puppet master

strings it along. You insist? – one
flick of your pinkie, one footfall on rock –
    it claps off. Its shadow
  is the only company it keeps.

The Same Complex System Can Contain Both Predictable and Unpredictable Behaviour; or, Two Views of a Squirrel

Trapeze artist, tumbler, high-wire act –
it never falters long enough for air
or leaf to let it down, never miscalculates
the velocity over the distance
a body must travel to bridge the gap, it
is the pippin that flouts Newton's laws,
the arrow whose trajectory
is divided and divided again, the messenger
dispatched from the scene of the battle
whose body count never hits the front page –

this one lay under the mailbox next door.
Reposed on its side, cheek on a cushion
of mulch. It was a glossy, well-exercised
Silicon Valley squirrel. My stomach
lurched. Tell me it's taking a break
the way birds stunned by their reflections do;
say it found this sweet spot to lie down and
listen to the background noises of every day:
sprinkler systems sprinkling as programmed; gears
crushing trash; next door that voice insisting
it be allowed to stay outside and play
for half an hour, just one minute more.

Early Spring, Wasatch Range

for Lucie

Larkspur arcs its downy spur, a girl in high heels
and not much else, parading in the violet mirror,
as we clamber upwards over boulders, rifts –
Indian paintbrush's scarlet claw, granite-embedded
sage brush weathered like the rails of a fence.
At the summit, under scrub oak unpacking new leaf
(back from another quick hop abroad),
we stare through crabbed, rust-scabbed limbs
at ants – horses, cows? – grazing on green sheets
laid out to dry in the basin, white on the far hills.

IN MY MOTHER'S GARDEN

Place Saint Sulpice

It rains on the roof of the church, fat
drops splat against zinc like overripe fruit.

In the Luxembourg yesterday: chestnuts
in bud. White clots fisted from sepals.

Today workmen file across the roof. North tower
girdled in scaffold. I can tell time by the manikin

who scales the toy-yellow crane at eight.
He enters the cab, the arm starts to tick.

If my thoughts had paws, they would make
strange marks in the snow.

My mother, alone. And who's to forgive?
I hide my feelings till I have no feelings

to speak of. 'Don't dramatise,' I tut my loves –
What is the ineradicable root of *love?*

Rain gurgles in gutters. A childhood sound.

At twelve o'clock, the crane stops. Egg yolk
against white: the sky blue-rinsed.

In Which, Years Later in Vancouver, We Watch a Movie Made in Saskatoon

At the bottom of the garden a flat brown ribbon,
the Saskatchewan, winds through prairie
to a city, where a woman picks sweet peas

and blows kisses at the camera. The sweet peas
smell like sweet peas fixed
by distant sunbeams; the sun – the same sun –

lights a border of salvia. Squeezed
into dad's den, we review this relic, on
video: effluvia of sweet pea

and nostalgia. The woman beautiful. A child
stumbles across the scene. Dad's overseas,
he hasn't seen his toddler. Was the movie for him?

You'd never guess there's a war on. Unscathed
people nod to the camera. Who
is the absent eye behind the camera?

The mother changes. The child scorched
around the edges – as if flesh could burn.
The grass is evergreen, but the river's

gone, the mother frowns. Snow fills the screen.
Under the garden's particles of light
mother says, can you rewind my river?

Power of Attorney

This is the gull's-eye view: strip mall
Vacationland, Vancouver Island.
Mother – a widow now – drives two cars
with her right foot on the gas
and her left foot on the brake.

And here they sit, Mother & Child
by some minor artist,
matched ankles demurely crossed,
the lawyer facing them, over
the deed in triplicate. 'Sign this,'

he scowls, down his specs
at my Munchkin of a mother,
'and your daughter can sell your house,
withdraw your savings –'
Hands in your lap. Don't fidget.
Keep a civil tongue in your head,
I'm thinking. Not the moment
for a joke. Low tide: salt water
rises to the boil in pots of sand;
oysters bang doors to their vaults.

Mother fixes me, perplexed: would
I sell the house from under her? Has
she overlooked a spot, like
a grease splotch on the stove,
in her incessant polishing, so that
when Death, of *Foreclosures Inc.*

knocks at the door again, trailed
by a couple of prospective buyers,
he'll find *nothing*
but sparkling countertops, sheets
pressed and filed away,
bills paid, even a nosegay
of fresh flowers – snapdragons, maybe –
nodding from the sea-chest in the entry?

'You see,' she says, with a bob
to her attorney, frown effaced,
the matter settled, eager to sign
her life away and move on
to the next item (the light bulb
for the oven) on the *To Do*
list for today – 'You see,' she says
to herself, 'she married a good man;
I trust he'll keep his thumb on her.'

And home we go, over French Creek
dad used to fish. Tide's turned.
Time to set aside old rancour,
I scold: Grow up! But – easier
said than done, and *love* – well –
love goes without saying. So I hold
my tongue and watch mother
negotiate the curves, coves round
into view between trees – madrone
bark smooth as infant skin. I catch
a whiff of seaweed drying

into wrinkles the tide will iron out.
I'll snip some cosmos
mother calls *come hithery*, and watch
the sea come up till only dull
slate nubs of rock
break the surface, like teeth,
while she does the dishes (*I know
how I like them*) and hangs
the laundry we left spinning
out.

Still Life with Peaches

Those three peaches
in the painting above the chest –
  something's wrong.

  Not the colour –
carnelian bleeding into gold –
  nor the shape –

  so dense with shade;
not the dusty texture of the skin
  like a cheek

  one dare not touch.
The flesh looks ripe enough to eat.
  No, no, it's

  how they're sitting
on the platter: hard, unforgiving –
  like apples.

Mother Weeding

Stooped over her perennial bed
on the rim of a cove the tide
comes each morning to clean, she weeds
towards the edge – a doe's leap
into nothingness – the sea's unsteady hands
forever buffing its grave goods.

Venus mound of a flowerbed,
a comforter on the cliff edge,
fragile, pulsing and oblivious;
blooms to wade into, clutching at names –
snapdragons, opium poppies,
lady's mantle in a web
of dewfall, cross-stitched
cushions of lavender, bees
tending to each floweret.
Did I say marigolds? Oh
well-behaved marigolds! Chins
up! Elbows tucked in!
Rue splatters the kitchen
window. Sea thrift. Spindrift.
Spendthrift? No – the sea
is a frugal housewife. The sea
recycles everything.

Private Property

The chipped-off, glued-back, washed
and rewashed crockery
of slate shines like household gods

a woman's dust cloth propitiates. Low tide.
A shelf of beach. The sun, rising,
torches roofs, flotsam-coloured

clapboard siding. The heron flaps off –
dad, I think,
revisiting his tide pools.

. . .

Fastened to the deer-proof fence
a sign: a primer
for the obstinate brambles –

> PRIVATE
> PROPERTY

Deer don't read. Lured
by mother's cornucopias
of butter beans, they trespass.

Nostalgia's dust cloth – I know –
puts a shine on everything, even
the quiet pain of quiet people,

and objects arraigned on tables
that sooner or later we'll take
to The Sale, for what on earth

are we to do with all these things we cannot keep
accumulating? Out from under
the fireweed, a raccoon and her cubs

glare at me. *Now what have I done?*
Bed not made? Porridge pot
left to soak in the sink? *Mother,*

of course. No sooner out of bed
these glorious August mornings
than she's at her mirror, eking out the ring

of eyebrows. Raccoon – I don't argue –
is my mother's spirit,
still cleaning up after me. Like wasp-waist

the Singer sewing machine (fibula of gold)
waiting to be collected for the Sale,
the hoe, the rake – all those other things

we won't be needing now
mother's found a smaller place,
and

> EVERYTHING
> MUST GO

Poem in Which I Pack You a Few Things for the Hospital

'Stop wasting electricity'

What if you walk in, what if
I don't hear the sound of the key,
and you catch me touching your things?
Undies, white on the left, right
silky black. Socks, six pairs, filed
according to colour, like Mendel
establishing the filiation of peas.
And here is your nightie: better
than the hospital's skimpy gown.
I lay it in the vanity case.

In the laundry – pressed into squares –
diapers you still use
to dust the veneer of nesting tables
and the helpless bric-a-brac gods.
I weep with the sound off as I was taught.
Promise, I'm not snooping – I unearth
the tin of shortbread, with fluted edges,
I steal two cookies. You won't mind
if I drink your cheap scotch. I pull
a few books off the shelf:
one marble flyleaf is inscribed
Jean P—, Saskatchewan, 1938:
Tennyson's *Complete Works*.

Doubt you'll miss it. One quick phone call.
At the ER you insisted:
Use the phone as much as you like,
then, fast, like dice
from a hand unexpectedly opened –
I'm sure glad you've come.
I shower, no one hears
the water tank emptying. Years
since I said my prayers – what
are these words that come unasked
to stammer at the knees of speech –

whose hand
taking the book, putting out the light?

The Down Syndrome Child

Blotch on the coach window? That's you
hurtling backwards through France.
You, the grotesque in the double glaze.
You, that tuneless droning, monotonous
as wind in a warped door.

Why stare through the high-tech glass
at outskirts trundled away? Pat
mama's cheek as if she might
solve the gap in your puzzle? Yes! Fire!
Point blank! Before she escapes!

Look – the sky is starting to fall.
Sheep browse in the dark-hedged pastures.
That trickle in the valley bottom
is old blood, it's a cut that won't heal.
It's *snow*: it effaces the details.

Trio Sonata for All Souls

Flute, harpsichord and violin –
the music's three voices join
– no, just one organ playing
all the parts, one musician's feet
and hands restless in the loft.

Some stained glass survives the wars.
The traceries look crocheted,
they look like the ivoried doilies
stored in an old chest of drawers.
Sitting on a rush-seat chair

bound to a row of rush-seat chairs,
you conjure up ghosts: carvers
of stone, makers of music, listeners
with lichened hands, following
trajectories of music and stone.

From his loft, the organist bows,
an old man with unruly hair –
the wind is blowing hard up there.
From the choir end, in a storm
of applause, a barn owl coasts
                    to its prayers.

Landscape with Laundry Drying

I say *dusk* and it obscures the boulders
dumped by glaciers an ice age ago.
The woman steps out of the boat, lets son
and husband tackle the moorings.
Balanced by groceries, she follows the harbour
round to their cottage, drops her bags
on the threshold and climbs to the lookout.
There's a line of laundry up there capering:
Jon's trousers, Tim's shirts, the striped blouse
she wore fishing yesterday. Her fingers
test for dampness still in the fibres, she
sniffs the salt air – stiff offshore breeze,
tattered cloud tumbling dry over Arranmore.
Channel flooded, inlets flooded – fullness
repairs the frayed edges of their island.

PS: Book of Eve

about that snake: it was beautiful,
truly
         it was beautiful
coiled on the cheek
of rock in early sun.
A garden snake, harmless therefore.
Bronze, I recall, frieze
of diamonds or black
down its sides or back
like great-uncle Sandy's
tartan socks.
One of life's lords,
Granddad wrestled
topsoil on his acre
of paradise. Beyond cedars
ocean sparkled. Stairs
descended to the first bright
beach of the world. Tide rising
or falling. It glittered
its tongue at me
and I will never forget
how it took me in, then
sashayed off
into the rough
where the berries hung.

Ⓑ editions

www.cbeditions.com